Life Goes on Inside Prison

Author: Bobby Bostic

Thanks to every prisoner who gave me a stamp

when I did not have one.

Thanks to every prisoner who helped me

when no one else cared.

Thanks to the prisoners who gave me food

when I had nothing to eat.

I feel your pain.

Thanks to the prisoners who kept me out of trouble

and the ones who were patient with me when I was

young and wild.

Thanks to the prisoners who keep on trying

when there seems to be no hope.

Keep trying until you find the right way

and do things right.

Never give up; Hard work pays off!

ISBN: 9780578688916

Book Categories: Crime, Social Science, Criminology

TABLE OF CONTENTS

The Redeeming Value of Art in Prison

Sometimes it is inside of the darkest places that we find the brightest light. However, the light is not always external. When the light comes from inside, it tends to shine for the whole world to see. This is why people are so amazed when they see the magnificent work of prison artists. Prison is raw and this is why the prison artist leaves his soul on the canvas. Whether the prison artist is writing, doing music, drawing or painting, they always express themselves in a soulful deep manner. It is like they are redeeming themselves from their past.

Prisoners tend to find atonement in their art. With limited resources, they find beauty in the ugliness that surrounds them. In the confines of prison art represents redemption. Art assists inmates in their quest of rehabilitation. Obviously, art has many redeeming qualities. Let's look at the word redeem. Redeem: (1) to free, or rescue by paying; (2) to free from the consequences of sin; (3) to convert into something of value; (4) to make good by performing; (5) to change for the better; (6) to atone for.

All six of these definitions are being manifested by the conscious prison artist as he is creating an artful masterpiece. Art is made in layers and must be uncovered by the person viewing it. Even the simplest of art evokes people to search for its deeper meaning.

Prison art screams out at you in many ways. It tells stories of longing, pain, need, wonder, beauty, and sometimes the divine. In creating such meaningful art, the prisoner finds meaning in their own life. This is how they redeem themselves. In many cases their talent is all that they have to give. While locked away in a cage, art allows them to free their souls. When outside patrons view their work, they have a voice. Art rescues the prisoner from obscurity. No longer just a number because their art expresses their humanity. Outside patrons make that connection with the prisoner's humanity.

With limited resources, prisoners get creative and make spellbinding art. When outside patrons view prison art, they wonder how could such talented artists commit such horrible crimes? Before they find the answer, the questions begin to answer itself through the prisoner's art. A prisoner knows that he can never take back his crime. He cannot undo his past. But this is where the term redeem comes into full play. By creating art that helps to heal other people, the prisoner is attempting to atone for his wrong. He is converting a mess into something of value. He is doing his best to make his life better by performing good art.

Bryan Stevenson once said that people are not the worst thing that they have ever done. This applies to prisoners also. Just look at their art. Before you write them off, let their art speak to you. What is the message? Feel it. Prison artists know that they have harmed society. They know that many people have been hurt by their crimes (including themselves). Therefore, they occupy their time in prison making meaningful art. In their art, they express remorse, warn others not to repeat their mistakes, and still see hope in a troubled world. Locked away from the world with all its problems, the prison artist still sees so much beauty in the world because more than anyone he knows, there is nothing like being free. For all its flaws, the world is still a beautiful place.

That's the picture the prison artist is painting or writing about. In the darkness of his prison cell, art beams down on his intelligence. Thus, he is guided through imagination and creativity to create a masterpiece. He hopes his art helps to heal someone's troubles. Through pen, paper, and canvas, the prison artist is trying to write his wrongs. All the while believing that the outside world can see the redeeming value of art in prison.

Life Goes On

Chapter 1

Life Goes On

Life goes on is a saying you will probably hear a lot, but nowhere does this saying have more significance than for people in prison. Their lives in the free world have ceased temporarily, but they have to live life in prison no matter how cruel that lifestyle might be. Time waits for no man. A prisoner's world does not have to be limited to prison, but it is the reality in which they are now at. The reader may ask what life is there to live in prison? It is not the greatest life, but nevertheless it is still a life. It must be stated for the record that prison is a world within itself. When people are sent away from society, they will create a world within the place that they are at. To occupy themselves and pass time, prisoners attend classes, go to religious services, play sports, talk on the phone, write letters, do artwork, watch television, read, and talk and joke among themselves. These things become a way of life for them inside of prison. Once a person is inside of prison, he or she has to accept that life on the outside world goes on without them. Then they must face the fact that they do have a life; they must live in prison no matter how much they may dislike that life.

In the general population of prison, an inmate finds things to do with his or her time. This keeps them busy and occupied. Life does indeed go on because prison is alive with energy and action. It is full of restless people with different personalities who have to find ways to keep their spirits up and relieve built up tension. Rather than thinking about the free world all day, they begin to create a life for themselves inside of prison. In fact, prisoners find ways to make life go on. They try to make the best of the worst.

I once heard someone say that, "prison in itself is not such a bad place; but it is the people in it that make it a bad place to be." After hearing this, I wondered to myself what could this saying possibly mean? Upon further analysis, I discovered that this saying means that prison is not always a bad experience because a person can make the best of it by changing their lives. A lot of prisoners lived life on the edge when they were in the free world. So, when many of them come to prison, they are offered a new start if they sincerely desire to change their lives. For this group of prisoners, life really does go on because they are ready to start a new life altogether when they are released from prison.

In prison when you wake up in the morning, you still attend to your hygiene and have some place that you are required to be. Even when you hate every minute of your existence in prison, you are still forced to go through the routines. Your day becomes based around a schedule. This schedule may vary from time to time or it can remain the same for years. It may seem like a very stupid schedule, but nevertheless it is still a schedule. Prison is a machine that must be constantly operated. A lot of prisoners just follow the programs that are already established and just go with the flow of the prison. The essence of it all is that they are still living. When a person goes to prison, life still continues on for them. Even in prison, life goes on.

Some of the World's Greatest Minds Are in Prison

Prison is a place where you can find scholars of every kind. The system can lock up a person's body, but they can't incarcerate our minds. Right here, we have some of the world's greatest minds. We have scientists, mathematicians, and preachers. In fact, many of you have excelled in the most difficult of all politics – prison politics. These politics can get deadly and messy. But people in here network to make things happen on scales great and small. We must continue to apply ourselves and not settle for a label that society has placed upon us.

The mind can accomplish what it will. It is stronger than concrete, razor, wire, and steel. The mind is an architect that constructs the plans that build the structures that house the institutions that change the world.

Throughout history, it has been right here in these prisons where scholars have used their minds to change the world. For documented evidence of this, we have the example of Nelson Mandela and how his words from his jail cell shook the world. It has been from these dungeons that some of the greatest words ever written have originated. These works came from the ink of a scholar's pen.

Look at the famous letter that Dr. Martin Luther King, Jr. wrote from the Birmingham jail cell that changed the course of the Civil Rights Movement and helped change the course of Kennedy's presidency. Angela Davis was interviewed in a California jail, inspiring a generation of Americans who wanted freedom for their communities. Paul wrote some of the New Testament of the Bible from a jail cell.

I declare today that some of the world's greatest minds are in prison. We can do what we put our minds to, and even these walls can't stop us. We can train ourselves to be legal scholars in order to obtain our freedom. We can get laws changed to benefit us. We can change this prison culture. All we have to do is put our minds and energy into it. Through self-rehabilitation, we can transform ourselves. I am not a model prisoner because prison does not model me. Still, I am determined to be the best that I can be.

We must not allow our talents to go to waste. We have to organize our creative energy with haste. The library is full of hundreds of books that we must start reading. Right there in the library, we can train ourselves to be scholars. We are not meant to be crooks. We are sitting in prison because we were not great criminals. But we are psychologists, accountants, and professionals of all kinds. The world has locked up some of its greatest minds. Once we tap into our own greatness, we can free ourselves from prison.

The smartest people do some of the dumbest things. That's how so many great minds end up in these prison wings. We came into prison as the problem, but now we can be the solution and help to heal the world. We have to succeed against the odds and claim the greatness that each of us possesses. It is from the lowest depths that greatest of people have risen. Some of the world's greatest minds are in prison.

The Myth of Rehabilitation

Chapter 2

The Myth of Rehabilitation

The theory of rehabilitation as being associated with prisons is a widely spread myth. Prison in itself is not a place of rehabilitation. It has to be up to the individual to want to rehabilitate him/herself. Within itself, prison is saturated with such ills and sickness that are designed to ill effect an individual. All across the country, prisons have changed their names to correctional and rehabilitation centers. The definition given for the word prison is a place for the confinement of person's in lawful detention, especially persons convicted of crimes; a place or condition of confinement or forceful restraint; a state of imprisonment or captivity. In accord with the objectives of modern law enforcement, prisons have been renamed or, so its purpose is supposed to be, for better reasons besides that of punishment. The aim of modern corrections is not supposed to be for the purpose of only punishing and housing inmates.

Modern corrections supposedly have the aim of rehabilitating prisoners and releasing them into society as changed people. Now let's look at the definition given for correctional centers. Correctional facilities are defined as a place of punishment intended to rehabilitate or improve, or the treatment of offenders through a system of penal incarceration, rehabilitation, probation, and parole. Surely this should be the purpose and end result of prisons. But on the contrary, prisons produce totally different results. Prison now days is more of a corporate business. Profits come before rehabilitation. Not only are prisons put on the stock market, but they are also in the private industrial and investment sector. The aim of corporations is profit and not rehabilitation. Prisoners become stock and trade in the free market. As such they are looked upon as monopoly capital. Their value is assessed at how much profit that they can produce and not so much as what contributions they can make to society as rehabilitated citizens.

In the absence of these rehabilitative classes and programs, the prisoners are left with idle time to sit around and brag on their past criminal exploits. We must ask ourselves what is it about prison that makes a person want to change? The answer simply is that prison in itself is not enough to make a person want to change. Harsh and restricted, an environment that prison is, it is not enough within itself to deter a person from engaging in criminal activities. Evidence of the above statement is the fact that today the Corrections Department has 68% recidivism rate. This means that 65% of prisoners will return to prison again once they are released.

The majority of prisoners do not just sit around and think of ways to change for the better. On the contrary, prisoners feed off of each other's criminal mentality. I was watching this television program the other day and one of the guests of the program called prisons a "University for Criminals." Before I could ask myself, what did she mean by this, she answered my question by commenting that "prison is a University of Crime because prisoners teach each other how to be better criminals." Say for instance, if in my neck of the woods we specialized in the crime of burglary. In the criminal world, this would be considered as petty crime. Nevertheless, burglary carries a sentence of 7 to 15 years. Now if I were convicted of this petty crime, I would be sent to prison with hardened criminals that are in for such crimes as robbery, murder, rape, extortion, etc. Being around these guys all day, of course I will learn about their past lives.

They will explain to me how many thousands of dollars that they were making off their crimes. In their explanation they will point out to me that their crimes were much more profitable and less risky than the crimes I committed. The criminal mentality feeds off this.

Within a few minutes of talking to them they have given me the entire blueprint on how to commit the crimes that were in their profession. A fellow prisoner can easily become your teacher in the criminal enterprise. Bragging on his or her criminal becomes the next prisoner's textbook on crime. Prisoners tell their stories with extreme passion. It is as if they are living the episode out again as they tell it to you. Their past is all that most of them have to look to. Therefore, they try to live in their past and some even refuse to change. Change or rehabilitation is a foreign concept to them.

Everyday prisoners learn new techniques to get over. Prison is such a place that it can turn a straight person crooked. There are so many rules that it is hard to not break them. And when you do try to follow all of the rules, you come into conflict with the other prisoners and you become an outcast among the outcast.

Prison only tames people, but it does not change people; at least not for the better. Psychological studies have proven how prison can have some devastating affects upon a person's psychosis and personality. This chapter and this book are not intended to give a psychological profile on prisoners and the mental effects that incarceration has on them. I have commented briefly on this subject to support my argument of dispelling the myth of rehabilitation in today's prisons. The government puts such illusory titles as correctional centers on the face of prisons to make it appear to the law abiding public that prison is really a place of change. Free citizens pay taxes for the maintenance and control of prisons and surely, they are concerned about the rehabilitation of prisoners. Statistics show that 60% of all prisoners will be released back into society. Free citizens are aware that many of these prisoners will be released back into the very communities in which they live so they should be concerned about the rehabilitation of these men and women in prison. The government justifies building more prisons to help control the public's fear of criminals. But in the end, prison helps to foster more criminals than it does to rehabilitate them.

Why is the recidivism rate so high? Why do prisoners keep returning to prison? It makes you wonder if these people like prison? No, they do not like prison. The problem sometimes comes as a result of prisons not having anything to offer that rehabilitates criminals. Taking people away from society and placing them in a cell is not going to rehabilitate them. Prisoners are not forced to go to any classes, with the exception of G.E.D. classes for those that are due to be released. Most prisoners opt not to go to these classes and programs because they see no purpose in attending these events. In their minds it is just a waste of time. Some of them look at the certificates given out at the completion of these programs as just a piece of paper. Not all prisoners look at it this way. In fact, many prisoners take pride in their accomplishments. In some cases, these certificates are all that some prisoners have to show for their accomplishments in and out of prison on a positive scale.

A person has to want to change in order for them to rehabilitate themselves. Prison can never rehabilitate the man; the man must rehabilitate himself. So, if an inmate is attending these classes for self-rehabilitative purposes then he or she is offered avenues to change their way of thinking as well as living. But the government is increasingly cutting these classes and programs due to budget constraints. The policy makers are not looking at the big picture because ultimately society loses more because these programs and classes are being cut. By cutting these programs, prisoners have lesser ways by which to rehabilitate themselves or even attempt to. It makes no sense for the government to take away from prisoners the few means that they have to rehabilitate themselves. This leaves them with nothing much to do but revert back to their old lifestyles. Prison is supposed to be a place of correction and therefore opportunities must be present within the prison that offers prisoners positive outlets and venues by which they can help themselves to change. When the government continues to remove these programs and classes, it is indirectly saying that it is not concerned with the rehabilitation of prisoners.

It is easy for someone to somewhat change while he is in prison. But in order to be actually rehabilitated, a man or woman must change his or her heart. Only then will that man or woman be able to reenter into society and not succumb to the temptations of his or her past and become a productive citizen in society. Prison does not change the person, but the person will alter his behavior while in prison. These men and women are under constant supervision all day. This serves as a deterrent for these men to stay out of trouble as much as they can while in prison. Therefore, they walk a thin line and many cases manage to stay out of trouble and keep a fairly clean record while in prison. All of this serves to further establish the myth of rehabilitation. Once these men are released from prison the myth of their rehabilitation quickly fades away. It becomes apparent that these men were not actually rehabilitated, but merely contained. Prison served to control these men while they were under confinement, but prison did not rehabilitate them.

Did the System Fail These Men Or Did These Men Fail the System

Who does the blame fall upon? Is it the system's fault or is it the fault of the prisoners who failed to be rehabilitated? The blame lies with both parties. But the major part of the blame goes to the system. Why? First and foremost, the system gives a false image to society as if prisons are correctional centers that are actually rehabilitating these men. Prison serves to control and lock away prisoners who would otherwise be in society vandalizing the property of business owners and corporations, and in some cases hurt people. Statistics show that the vast majority of prisoners are incarcerated for non-violent crimes. Who benefits from the government giving society the notion that prisoners are actually being rehabilitated while in prison? In the end, big business and corporations make mega profits from the incarceration of prisoners while society and the prisoners end up losing.

Everyday a new prison is being built somewhere for the purpose of locking down and confining human beings. There are more prisons being built than schools all over the world.

The myth of rehabilitation is very much alive and well. The government shows favorable statistics that serve its political ends giving the appearance that crime is declining due to low recidivist rates as if prisoners are actually being rehabilitated. In reality, recidivism rates are actually on the rise. The government will keep alive and thriving the myth of rehabilitation because it serves government purposes. The construction of thousands of new prisons every year must be justified in the eyes of tax paying citizens. In conclusion, I ask the reader to consider all that I have said here. Prison within itself does not rehabilitate people and we must not be duped

by the myth of rehabilitation.

Everyday Rituals

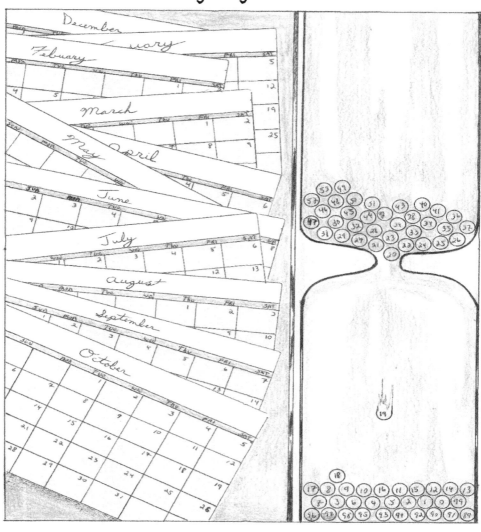

Chapter 3
Everyday Rituals

Prison life is very mundane. In fact, living in prison consist of the greater part of going through everyday rituals. The majority of inmates in prison have close-circuited minds so instead of taking advantage of the numerous programs and other outlets that are available, they get caught up in the same everyday rituals. Today's modern prisons are very sociable environments. Therefore, many inmates spend their time indulging in aimless gossip. The concept of prison being a place of rehabilitation is a myth. (I will discuss this in detail in a later chapter). Many of the everyday rituals that prisoners find themselves engaging in is oriented toward the same behavior patterns they displayed on the streets. From the music they listen to down to their style of dress, many prisoners attempt to keep their street affiliations alive and well. Many of them operate out of the same street mentality tailored to a prison environment. In their minds and attitudes, nothing will change them or their way of thinking; not even a harsh atmosphere such as prison will suffice to do this job. Their street lifestyles somewhat pre-conditioned them for a future in prison. No sane person wants to be in prison. When you are steeped in the street mentality, you indirectly confine yourself to a prison. Living this sort of lifestyle finds a person engaged in the same everyday rituals just as a person in prison does.

No doubt, prison is a very boring and sad place, but at the same time it is only what you make of it. A progressive prisoner takes the few available opportunities and finds ways to better him/herself. Even if a progressive prisoner is stuck with the everyday rituals that make up prison life, he or she will not confine themselves to the same mundane schedule of an ordinary prisoner that is not conducive to progress. On the contrary a progressive prisoner will find or even create alternative ways to develop themselves and become better citizens. They are able to think outside of the box.

The everyday rituals of prison life are not progressive. In fact, the mundane activities of prison life are not progressive and not geared toward success. This is why prisons and so-called correctional centers are not places of re-habilitation. They are the very opposite of that.

Waking up everyday going through the same futile rituals of the prison cycle can be accurately described as "going through the motions." For a complete discovery on why we have to look at an outline of an ordinary schedule for a prisoner confined to an institution, I will give an accurate description of a typical schedule for a prisoner.

The beginning of the ritual typically begins with the pre-dawn custody count at around 6 a.m. in the morning. The custody count is when the institution makes its five daily headcounts to make sure that each inmate is present at the institution. Shortly after count, inmates are allowed to go eat breakfast, or in some cases have it brought to them. After everyone has eaten breakfast, the prison comes alive with activity. There are numerous programs and outcounts that prisoners are allowed to attend. A brief overview of the programs and classes that are established within the institutions in this country consist of: substance abuse class, AA, Thinking for Change, Breaking Barriers, Restorative Justice, Victims Impact Class, G.E.D., Life Skills, Vocational Tech classes, and other such programs. Also, there are the various workplaces that operate in practically every prison in this country. There are such jobs as the furniture factory, chemical plants, warehouses, license plate factories, laundry, maintenance, canteen, etc.

Out of all the above-named classes, programs, and jobs that I have named, only a small percentage of the prison population are allowed to attend and gain employment. The rest of the prisoners are left with idle time on their hands. Their everyday rituals then consist of playing cards, engaging in fruitless conversations, and reminiscing about their past street life. Prison is a place where inmates entertain each other on a constant basis. In this way, they can escape the harsh realities that have set upon their life. Gossip is a favorite past time of the average prisoner.

Again, the daily schedule of an ordinary prisoner consists of being awakened at the pre-dawn custody count. Then after eating the breakfast meal, the day begins. Some prisoners go straight to work and others to their various classes and programs. Usually they remain there until lunch time, then they are released to lunch and back to their cells for custody count. After lunch, if they still have more classes or programs, then they will return there or either back to their place of employment within the prison. They will usually remain there until around 3 or 4 o'clock in which time they return to their cells for another custody count. After count, inmates are allowed to go eat dinner in the same dining hall in which they ate their earlier meals of breakfast and lunch; or in some cases food is brought to their living areas. Following the super meal, prisoners are allowed some recreation time to play ball, lift weights, and various other recreational activities. A small percentage of inmates will take this time to go to their religious outcounts, many of which are held at nighttime. Usually after these activities are partaken in, it is time for lockdown at night in which inmates must stay confined to their cells until the next day, unless they are workers. The above paragraphs have given a fairly accurate description of the average schedule of a prisoner.

Of course, there are various exceptions for the few progressive prisoners who choose to take advantage of every opportunity available and create alternative ways of occupying themselves. These prisoners do not blindly or unconsciously follow the everyday rituals of prison life. On the contrary, their horizons extend beyond the boundaries of the prison. As the saying goes, "You can lock up my body, but you cannot lock up my mind." In other words, these prisoners find within prison life creative ways to better themselves and humanity as a whole.

Engaging in everyday rituals is not something that defines their life. The books that they read help them to escape the prison they were living in on the streets. Being in prison offers them ample time to read and a wise prisoner takes advantage of this opportunity. Many prisoners get in tune with their spiritual side while they are in prison. The books that they read could be self-help books or career-oriented books. Reading is a world of its own and it helps the prisoner to go to a world beyond what he or she ever knew existed before they came to prison. Via their extensive reading, they are learning other people's experiences as well as gaining valuable information on how to start and develop their careers once they are released from prison. So, although they may be forced to go through many of the everyday rituals of being in prison, they do not allow their minds to become confined to the prison. An everyday ritual for them is just another way to better themselves. For the creative prisoner, there is always another way to use their time for self-improvement.

In its most immobilized state, an everyday ritual in prison can consist of nothing more than thinking, using the bathroom, eating, and talking. The fruit reaped from the seed of that thinking finds its worth based on the quality and nature of the thoughts that the thinker is contemplating upon. If the thinker was evaluating his/her life in a positive light and focusing upon changing character flaws, then such an everyday ritual can surely produce positive results. It is thought that leads to actions and if a person is continuously thinking about positive things, then those thoughts should manifest themselves through positive actions.

Even for the most progressive type of prisoner, the everyday rituals of prison life can become a burden. Why? Because it seems like you have to look forward to the same things every day. Having many activities in your schedule still consist of something that you have probably already done before. Since prison is designed as a place of punishment, it is probably supposed to be boring, but in order to take on the title of correctional center or rehabilitation facility, it should not be so mundane as to have the same everyday rituals that fail to reform prisoners and keep them stagnant in life. There is no use in any man following an everyday ritual if that ritual does not have any substance. It is a waste of time. From experience I know that prison does not have to be a waste of time if the prisoner chooses to occupy him/herself. A prisoner must become progressive and make his everyday rituals in prison consist of activities that are geared toward self-improvement. Otherwise the average prisoner will continue to remain to be among the blind prison masses going through the motions of empty everyday prison rituals.

Sport and Play

Chapter 4
Sport and Play

S port and play are the main two activities that take place inside of prisons. Regardless of the terrible conditions and other tensions that saturate the atmosphere, these two activities take precedence over everything else. Why? It is because these two activities help to occupy the prisoners and keep the more serious and stressful things off of their minds. The definition given for play in the dictionary is (1) to occupy oneself in amusement, sport, or other recreation; (2) to take part in a game; (3) to participate in betting, gambling; (4) to act in jest or sport; (5) to behave carelessly or indifferently; (6) to behave or converse in a sportive or playful way. The above description has given an accurate overview of the daily activities of many prisoners. However, this definition would not be complete without a definition of the word sport, which is defined as: (1) an active pastime, a form of recreation; (2) mockery, jest; (3) a joking mood or attitude; (4) to joke or trifle; (5) to display or show off.

The average law-abiding person in the free world would think that prison is a serious place. To a certain extent it is, but only under certain circumstances. For the most part, prisons are passive. Prison is a very sociable environment. More gossip is exchanged in prison than anywhere else in the world. People in free society would think that people who are in prison spend most of their time trying to get out, but when you are on the inside, you know that prisoners spend more time concerned with what is going on inside of the prison. Humans in general have a tendency to focus on the world that they are in; especially people who are incarcerated. Inmates spend so much time isolated that they take advantage of every opportunity that they get to mingle. During the time they are confined to their cells, they are left with nothing but their thoughts, imagination, and sometimes the television and radio. Most prisons allow inmates time throughout the day for recreation periods. During this time, prisoners are allowed to exercise on the yard, play basketball, jog around the track, lift weights, play games, and just stand around on the yard. There is a portion of the prison population who do not exercise at all. Oftentimes, the majority of prisoners rotate among each other in working out and playing games as well as sports.

In this stagnant environment, prisoners must entertain themselves. Since many of them are dealing with a lot of stress and pressure, they tend not to focus on the more serious things, and they spend their time engaging in sport and play. This keeps them in a passive mode. Their menial jobs do not require much skill or focus. So even in the prison workplace they are free to indulge in constant buffoonery without any repercussions. Instead of waking up mad and stressed out about being in prison, many inmates wake up to a pre-arranged schedule which in turn allows their minds to be focused on the day ahead of them. If they are entertained with their jokes and blabber, they are not keeping themselves stressed out about their conditions in prison. By jesting and keeping a jolly attitude, they are not walking around stressed out focusing on the more critical aspects of their situation.

When people can find something to laugh and joke about every day, they do not have to focus on the more serious problems in their life. In prison, sport and play are the main forms of escapism. Many prisoners are under the impression that all they have to look forward to is their next parole date or the answer back from their court appeal.

Of all the things to do in the world, why would prisoners choose to play? Because as long as people are playing and jesting there is no worry. Just as the definition explains that I gave earlier of play, prisoners take on a careless and indifferent attitude. If you were just an average reasonable observer of a modern maximum prison, you would be shocked to find out the extravagant sentences that the inmates have. Through observation a person would be left with the impression that a prisoner serving a life sentence is going home tomorrow. Why? Because they act so carefree and happy. To escape the harshness of their reality, they even make the more serious things of life into a game. This is how they suppress their anger and channel their energy.

The library and educational departments are the less frequented places of prison. The recreation areas and card tables are the most crowded and favorite hangouts of the majority of inmates. Wherever there is amusement going on is where the average prisoner can be found. Most prisoners are not political, and for the ones who are not serious about life, intellectual debates for them are just another form of entertainment.

Through sport and play prisoners are afforded the opportunity to release built up tension. Thus, through this entertainment, they are stuck in the same repetitive cycle. There are so many games that prisoners play. From mind games to playing the freaks, they do it all. Playing the freaks is prison slang for gay jokes. Many prisoners do this all day and think nothing of it. Playing the freaks in the extreme consist of touching, patting, and feeling on one another. Many of these men are not active homosexuals, but they still play the freaks to pass time. For the ones that are actually homosexuals, playing the freaks is their main form of entertainment. Yes, prison can sometimes be a sick place.

Free society will be surprised at the games that prisoners play with each other. There seems to be no limit or boundaries to these games. When men can sit around and exchange homosexual jokes with one another all day, this is a clear testament of their level of development. This may be shocking to the reader, but most prisoners just look at it as clean fun. The reader may ask how can grown men sit around and play homosexual name game calling all day? The answers that are given by prisoners who do play these games hardly make any sense. If they are asked why they play these games, they will just tell you that it is just something that they do to pass time or that they only play the freaks with people that they know and that it is no harm in it.

The above just goes to show the wasteful state of prisons today. Underneath all of the order is chaos. Sport and play seem to be the order of the day. Of course, this playful environment in such a place as prison can have its setbacks. Play in prison can sometimes turn deadly. You can find more comedians in prison than anywhere else in the world. These men are starved for attention and will get it anyway they can. The prison administration uses this psychological stronghold as a weapon against the prisoners.

When men who are incarcerated are kept pacified by sport and play all day, they are not dealing with real life issues that caused them to come to prison in the first place. They are still suffering from the same mental diseases. Prison can make these mental diseases even worse because prison can definitely be a sick environment at its core. Not to deviate from the topic at hand, though being incarcerated in prison is definitely stressful. The stress merely lingers. It cannot be escaped in the end. But nevertheless, inmates will do anything in their power to do so. Not wanting to go to administrative segregation, visiting restrictions, denial of recreational privileges, parole setbacks, etc. keep prisoners tamed and out of trouble. Their main problems are never dealt with. Underneath, many of them are still not dealing with their core issues.

In life, sport and play have their purposes, but in prison this should not be the order of the day. The prison administration does not have a problem with this as long as the prisoners are contained. Their only job and concern are the order and security of the prison. They do not worry about the long-term effects that this will have on society.

As long as prisoners engage in sport and play, they are not forced to deal with their real problems in life, and as such they are not forced to accept responsibility for their crimes. Neither will they be inclined to change their way of thinking. Serious goals for the future are not set and striven after. Real change is never accomplished. Kids play because they do not have any real responsibility in life. When men play all of the time, they are neglecting their responsibilities as men no matter where they may be. There must be a balance between being serious and engaging in sport and play. Without this balance, prison will continue to remain a revolving door. Prisoners must become more serious about life and their present situations. Prison must become a place of change and not a place of games.

Living Television Fantasies

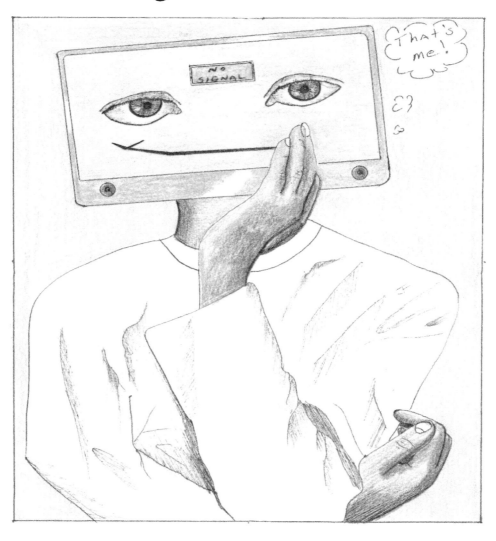

Chapter 5
Living Television Fantasies

Prison, per se, more than any other place in the world is where human beings live out their fantasies via the television. Tell-a-vision is an easy world to get caught up in. In a lot of ways, television is prisoners only visual access to the outside world. They begin to see the world through the television, although in many cases what they are seeing is not the real reality. The majority of time, the world they are viewing through the television is not in conjunction with the world they were living in before they went to prison, nor the world that they will be dealing with when they are finally released from prison. Today's television shows present no real substance to its viewers. On the contrary, today's television market consists of what caters to the lower base of human being's passions. Besides this, television is controlled by big corporations and the media is just an outlet to sell products and ideas. These products and ideas extend from everyday household needs to vulgar sex. In fact, sex sells, so even when a corporation is trying to sell innocent household products, it will advertise through a sexy commercial. I am not going to go into a long discussion about the evils of television and how the media uses subliminal seduction to capture the minds of the masses (i.e. its viewers). But what I intend to do is illustrate how the prisoners use television to subliminally seduce themselves and live in a fantasy world via the television.

The evils of TV have a great effect upon prisoners in particular and on people in institutions in general. I mentioned earlier the fact that sex sells, and the media has found television to be the greatest place to sell sex. The viewer no longer has to go to obscene adult channels to see explicit sex. Most cable channels and even regular television stations air shows that have a high sexual content to them. No one group or population of people is more forcefully deprived of sex than human beings who are confined to prisons and other institutions. Therefore, television is the perfect outlet for them to live out their sexual fantasies. Also, since sexually oriented shows and movies are repeatedly aired on television, prisoners have an unlimited diet of sexual fantasies. Even the most moral and upright prisoner will succumb to such television fantasies. Nowadays it is hard to watch television in an innocent manner because almost everything on television has a sexual tone to it. Mostly this is done because television producers are well aware of the fact that sex sells, and they use this to their advantage to generate a greater profit.

Sex is not the only fantasy that prisoners attempt to live out via the television. There are thousands of fantasies that prisoners attempt to live out via the TV. Not all of them are bad either. In fact, some of them are used for inspiration. But for the most part, the television fantasies that prisoners attempt to live out are harmful to themselves and keep them stagnant as well as stuck in a frame of mind detrimental to their progress. For instance, when prisoners see the rich and famous on television, they sit back and wish they could have these things, but most of them do not have the motivation or determination to do what it takes to get these things. So, like the average person they sit back and envy the more fortunate people who have these things. Just because a person is blessed and well off, every bad thing that can be imagined in the jealous person's mind will be attributed to the former. Envy can take on murderous proportions.

Prisoners tend to live out the wildest fantasies through televisions. This is not to say that ordinary free citizens do not have wild fantasies. Nothing is more impressionable upon the mind than a picture. When you put that picture with color, sound, and motion, it leaves an impressionable effect upon the mind. Since prisoners are not in the free world, they tend to absorb every detail and scene from the programs that they see on television. This is their connection and proof of what is going on in the world. After years of living television fantasies while in prison, it only takes a week or less for prisoners to realize that they were in fact living television fantasies while they were in prison. The real world paints a totally different picture than the one that was painted on the television.

People in prison wish that they were free so in their own way through the television, they see themselves right out there living in the free world with everyone else. The reader may ask is there anything wrong with this. Can there possibly be any harm in a person in prison imagining themselves free via scenes that they see on the television screen. Of course not. The problem enters when prisoners get caught up in a make-believe world that prevents them from facing their reality or attempting to change it. The fantasies that most of them live in through the television will never materialize. Therefore, instead of them wasting valuable time living television fantasies, that time could be used by them taking a deeper look at their characters, thinking patterns, and trying to change themselves for the better. When they spend most of their time watching television, they merely transfer their patterns of thinking and character traits unto the images that they try to live out based upon what is portrayed upon the television screen. What is the effect of this? For them it means that they stay stuck in the same mind frame or digress to an even worse state than before they entered prison. This happens because they are trying to live in the world of television, which is not the same as the real world, they are living in. So, in essence inmates try to mentally escape from prison by means of living out their television fantasies. Sometimes we all wish to live in a world different from the one that we actually live in. But if a person sits around all day trying to live in a virtual fantasy world, then they will remain stuck in time and a position that is not progressive.

In prison, television is the ultimate commodity. For most prisoners it is a must have, but the misuse of it can have damaging effects. When the television becomes a prisoner's world when he or she wakes up in the morning, the first thing they do is turn on the television. It can get to the point where they unconsciously worship that television. The television becomes their programmer. They base their day and schedule around what is on television.

One cannot base his world around fantasies and be prepared to face the real world. Reality becomes harsh to them and some people do not know how to deal with this, while some others are used to it. For those that do not know how to deal with it, their worlds become crushed. All of the illusions they built for themselves are destroyed within a very short time. Where does this leave them? We cannot necessarily say that this leaves them unfit for society because there are a lot of people in free society who erroneously attempt to live out their life through television fantasies. For the prisoner who has been away from society for so long, to have to come home and find a world totally opposite from the one he or she pictured through the television can have very damaging psychological and emotional effects. The restricted environment of prison they just left had them suffering from numerous psychological and emotional scars as is, and to build up a screen or refuge from this by creating television fantasies for themselves, only to have them destroyed when they enter the free world, leaves them totally unbalanced.

Once faced with the realities of the real world, the prisoners can find themselves off balance and unprepared to deal with the real challenges that awaits them. TV is so mesmerizing that it is easy to get caught up in its illusions. As I pointed out earlier, many people in prison choose to occupy their time by watching television. But the real world is not structured in a way for them to actually carry out these fantasies. They will only get frustrated in the process of attempting to live out such television fantasies and therein lies the danger of these fantasies. In conclusion of this chapter, I must again emphasize the fact that it is detrimental and unhealthy for prisoners to indulge in a constant diet of television. Prisoners need to feed their minds with healthier images and use their time to try to change their realities through positive actions and hard work.

Institutionalized

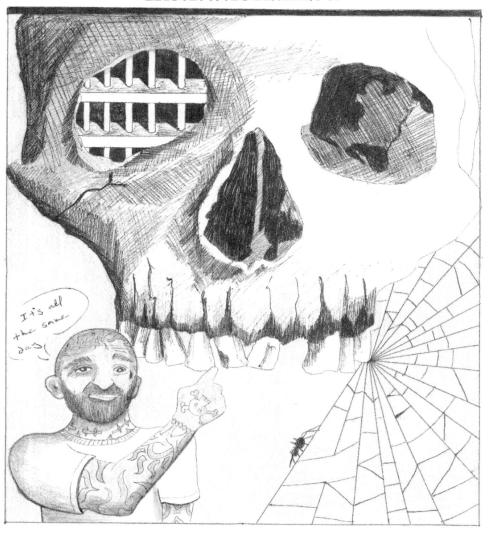

Chapter 6

Institutionalized

Prison can only confine a person within its boundaries, but it doesn't necessarily confine their minds. When a person allows prison to confine their minds, they become institutionalized. The dictionary (Oxford's Advanced Learner's Dictionary, Fifth Edition) defines the term institutionalized as: "to make a person accustomed to living in an institution, so as to lose their ability to think or act independently." There is a deeper definition to this term that a definition in the dictionary cannot adequately and completely explain. To become institutionalized means to be limited to a certain type of thinking based around a particular lifestyle, i.e. in this scenario – prison. Just because a person is confined to an institution does not mean they have to become institutionalized. This itself is only a form of escape for the weaker minded person who doesn't want to live life outside of the box. Therefore, he or she graduate from the institutionalization of the street life to becoming institutionalized to an actual institution. His or her whole life revolves around their thinking and living in prison. They start to view the whole world in this light. It doesn't take a person a long time to become institutionalized. It depends on the strength of their mind and their determination to do something in life.

A follower is a primary candidate to become institutionalized within a short period of time.

Prison is definitely an environment of the blind leading the blind. A follower is someone that will follow the masses, and since a great majority of prisoners are already institutionalized, a follower will just blend in with the prison mass. It is easy to become institutionalized, but it is very difficult to grow out of that mind-set once it sets in. Once the person is released from prison, they will find themselves still institutionalized. They will approach life on the streets from a prison angle. The sad part about it is that they do not even realize they are institutionalized, and if someone insists that they are, then they will vehemently argue otherwise.

Institutionalization is not just a term, but a disease. Once inside, it attacks a person and it is a die-hard mentality; like a virus, it has to be fought off. It extends beyond the life of the institution and permanently shapes the person's views on life in general. Even when they are released to the streets, they operate out of mind frame as if they are still in an institution. They will easily find themselves communicating with people in the free world the same way that they communicated with inmates at the institution they were in. This is because once a person becomes institutionalized, they begin to operate on this basis no matter where they may be. Rather it is at a place of business, in their homes, at work, etc., this mentality pervades their thinking.

One of the worst results of a person becoming institutionalized is when they are released and have to deal with authority figures. They operate from an incarcerated mind frame. Such as when they are at work, they look at their bosses as the police, which is a result of the constant harassment they received from correctional officers. Any person who is in authority over them becomes looked upon as an enemy. Although it is a terrible symptom of a person being institutionalized, it is also natural for the average human being to dislike anyone who takes advantage of their authority position over them. Of course, with a person who is institutionalized, his or her hate towards all authority figures, in most cases, amounts to extremism. In the eyes of that person, people with authority positions represent the system and that system is their ultimate enemy. The institutionalized person is so blinded by their hate of the system that they fail to see people as ordinary people when these people happen to be employed by the system.

As I emphasized earlier; the word institutionalized is not just a catchy phrase, but it is more of an accurate description of a disease. It is the sort of mentality that has lifetime side effects. Once affected with this mental disease, the carrier does not even detect its effects upon their thinking and way of viewing life. It attacks the way that they see life on all fronts. It eats away at them and confines their thought process to a limited programming based on their experiences at whatever institution that they were at. Even thirty years after their release from prison, people can still find themselves institutionalized to a certain degree. Like I said before, it is a mental disease that spreads itself and takes a stronghold on the mental department. After a person overcomes many of its side effects, there are still many areas of their life where it still has a great influence.

You cannot look at a person's body language and determine whether or not that person is institutionalized. You cannot listen to their tone of speech and figure out if they are institutionalized. Neither can you look at everyone who has been released from prison or any other institution as being classified as being institutionalized. Believe it or not, you have millions of people in the free world who have never stepped foot into a prison or any other institution, but nevertheless they are more institutionalized than persons who have been in institutions for years.

Institutionalization comes as a result of people having one track minds and only dealing with life and people in the world based on a level of thinking they limit themselves to as a result of their limited experiences in the limited world they confine themselves to. Institutionalization is not based on a particular way of doing things. Just because a person follows a certain schedule on a daily basis does not make them what you call institutionalized. It would require more of a scientific explanation to draw out in detail what it means to be institutionalized. This was merely an attempt to explain to the average layperson what the term means. Furthermore, a complete reading of this book will give the reader a detailed description overall of what it means for a person to become institutionalized. The contents of this chapter are intertwined with the other chapters to make this book a whole. All of the subjects tie in with each other or pick up from where other chapters left off. The meaning and description of the term institutionalized is indirectly explained throughout the book.

Religion In Prison

Chapter 7
Religion in Prison

R eligion: this word has many definitions, and in this chapter I will attempt to explain how this world relates to prisoners and their lives. The word "religion" comes from the Latin religare, meaning to bind together (ligare) again (re). The dictionary lists several definitions, defining it as belief in a divine power, and/or expression of this belief, plus a unique system of belief (sacred or profane), a way of life. So, despite the many definitions that I will list for this word, it boils down to a way of life. Religion is a personal thing for each of us. There can be several stages of religion that we go through. It becomes the truth and light of our life. For some of us, this truth can signify an illusion that we are trying to make a reality or waiting in the darkness of a profane life trying to find a light in a way of life that only produces darkness. Now this last definition given is a perfect explanation of what religion is to most prisoners. Since religion is a way of life, it can be explained as sacred, spiritual, or vulgar, depending on which particular religion or way of life a person adheres to. For some people, their religion is simply having fun. Religion is supposed to be a serious thing, but how can some people take their religion serious when they do not even take life seriously?

The surprising thing is that in prison you will find some of the most serious converts of religion. They are seriously devoted to the tenants of their religion. And the first question that people ask is, why do people go to jail in order to find God? Is that a mock question or not? It is a serious question that people often ask. Even the prisoners themselves ask this question. The rebellious prisoners defy this theory altogether. When asked why they have not found God, they will say that they were not on the street trying to be holy so why would they come to prison and try to be holy. In retrospect they say that they will find God when they get around to it or when the time is right (which may never be). There is a sizable population of agnostic prisoners as well. As for those who are in doubt, they will say if there is a God why does He allow the world to be in the terrible condition that it is?

The prison class is one of the most oppressed class of people on earth. The oppressed people look to God to rescue them from the oppression of tyrants. So naturally they will implore the assistance of God and try to confirm their lifestyles to His will. Plus, they come to a point in their life in which they realize that they are powerless, and they need help with their problems in life. In short, they need a savior and they look for it in religion.

Prisoners also come to realize that they have been oppressing themselves for years. Thus, in this state of feeling, they will blame themselves for their present condition. Drugs could not free them from themselves. Many of them turned to drugs to escape from their conditions. Drugs became their religion and way of life. But in the end, drugs were not fulfilling enough to fill the empty void in these people's lives. Furthermore, drug use lead to the commission of other crimes in order to finance their drug habit. For others, it was trying to live a fancy lifestyle that caused them to come to prison. Wealth and partying were their religion. It seems that all people do something to fulfill themselves or make themselves feel complete. There are no known people without some form of religion, no matter how simple its way of life and thought.

What happens when all of these artificial religions fail? In the end, people have to turn to the true source of light which is God. He has been described as the greatest source of peace and perfection. And what is it that we all seek in one way or another? Peace and perfection are what we seek. Our drug highs give us some sort of ultimate release and we feel perfect in this state. This is what getting high consist of for us. When people go to prison, their world is turned upside down. They reach the lowest of the low, even lower than the period of their desperate drug binges. Still they desire to see the light. They try a lot of ways to do this only to find that many of these things don't work. In the end, they reach the conclusion that God is their ultimate savior and the only one that can rescue them from the inner turmoil they are experiencing. Therefore, they turn to God. Now of course you will find many fake or insecure converts in prison. Prison is full of self-made hypocrites. Some of the worst kind of religious hypocrites are in prison.

Sincere and Insincere Conversion While In Prison

Conversion to God is not just something that happens overnight. There is a great deal of people who experience sincere conversions while they are in prison. As I indicated earlier, prison is such an environment that it exposes a person to their helplessness and the need for a higher power in their life. Prison offers people a lot of free time to read, and what better books to read than spiritual books. Everywhere you look in prison you will see a Bible or Quran. These religious texts get read very often in prison. Prisoners have much time to reflect and ponder on the verses of these Holy Scriptures. Since prison is such a restricted environment it makes it easier for these men and women to practice their religious tenants.

Why would someone fake with God? Being a hypocrite and being amongst hypocrites for so long, hypocrisy starts to become second nature to some people. While others just ask for forgiveness at regular intervals and figure that soon enough that will get their life right with God. They even convince themselves that God understands why they commit certain sins. A prisoner's favorite excuse as to why he or she sins is the fact of their circumstances being in prison. Many converts to religion want to have their cake and eat it too. Meaning that they want to live their secular life also. We all fall short of perfection, especially in the area of religious conversion. So, even the best of us can display actions that reap of hypocrisy in the eyes of the beholder.

Religion has to offer a constant feeling of truth for its adherents or religion losses its appeal. A sincere conversion to religion is one in which a person truly discovers God and His relation to them as well as the universe. Once this is discovered wholly, a person has virtually experienced a religious conversion. It is not just a feeling though; it is more of a life changing experience. Once a person comes into this experience their entire view on life is changed. Therefore, their behavior and thinking patterns change.

There is a small portion of prisoners who get released into society and remain true to their religious tenants. Their religious conversion in prison was a true and sincere one. But what about those prisoners who are very religious while in prison, but revert back to their old criminal lifestyles once they are released to the streets? Was their religious conversion sincere? Sometimes only God and that person truly know if their conversion was sincere or not. As for those pure sincere religious conversions that take place while a person is in prison will show in the person's way of living. There are thousands of religious conversions that take place daily in prisons across the world.

A Profane Religious Life

Profane means something that is not sacred, something that is vulgar, blasphemous, irreverent, or profane talk or behavior. Many people in prison live a very profane religious life. Profanity is some people's entire way of life. Prison can be such a dismal environment at times that you will hear some of the most vulgar conversations that a man can think of. A lot of guys in prison are so negative that their entire outlook on life is negative. This negativity doesn't just remain with them, but they extend it to everything that they see in the world. Most prisoners lived a profane religious life before they came to prison and get worse with it when they go to prison.

Some people's fetishes become the God that they worship. And in prison, fetishes easily become a stumbling block in people's lives. Their life revolves around their fetishes and in a sense, they get stuck there. Usually when we speak of fetishes, we think of something sexual. Every fetish is not of a sexual nature.

Prison can put man in his lowest state, and in such an animalistic state, man is subject to do almost anything. Many prisoners live profane religious lifestyle because they are living in their lowest state (animalistic state). There are no moral codes to this lifestyle. Prison then becomes a jungle worse than the jungle on the streets. In prison, you have the wildest of the street jungle, and when you combine all of these elements together it can produce chaos. Those who garner the most respect is the most profane. They surely get the most attention. Those who are the most positive and keen on living a sacred religious life are the most alienated. The surprising thing about prison though is the sincere religious converts are highly respected in prison. The most profane prisoner respects the sincere religious convert. He is respected because of his discipline and dedication to his religion. Even fools respect knowledge and the sincere religious convert in prison usually does a lot of studying and via his studies he acquires a lot of knowledge and prisoners respect knowledge more than anything else next to violence.

New inmates or veteran inmates usually do not go against the grain of what is going on in prison. The happenings of prison is of a profane nature. There prisoners believe in God, but their faith in God is not strong enough to make them abstain from their profane lifestyles.

In conclusion, I must quote something that I read awhile back which said that "numerous critics changed that many religious doctrines had become dry and uninspiring and no longer satisfied spiritual needs. Critics also claimed that traditional religions failed to deal with current social issues and that they supported outdated moral attituded." From another source, I read a definition given for religion as it "could rightly be described as man's response to the exigency of the human condition, in which he is driven to seek security, status, and permanence by identifying himself with a reality greater and more durable than himself." Both of these descriptions have embodied in short what I said throughout this chapter. This chapter was not meant to give a theological overview of the conditions in the world's prisons. Again, I have merely attempted to give the most accurate description that I could pertaining to religion and its overall place in the prison environment.

How the Guards
Abuse Their Authority

Chapter 8
How the Guards
Abuse Their authority

G aurds in modern prisons are tentatively called C.O.'s, which is an abbreviation for Correctional Officer. Throughout this text though, I have referred to them as guards as a more accurate description of their title. Their duty and job in the prison is strictly for security purposes. They are there to oversee the prisoners. The average prison houses around 2,000 inmates. Any given housing unit contains about 300 inmates. There are only about 4 or 6 guards assigned to each house for 8-hour shifts. Almost all of the inmates have needs or places that they have to go and therefore they have to interact with the guards in some manner. Everything requires patience in prison. With all of these frustrated men in one place dealing with various problems and issues can cause prison to be a tense and stressed environment at times. This stress can rub off on guards shortly after their employment at prison.

Everything that goes on among the prisoners, the guards have to deal with it in one way or the other. So, for the 8 hours that the guards are at work, the prison becomes a part of their life. For the most part, the ratio of inmate against guard violence is very low. Most incidents recorded of guard assaults are not those that cause serious bodily harm. The consequences of assaulting a guard is severe. In almost every case that an inmate causes harm to a guard of serious or even not so serious nature, that inmate will be subject to prosecution. In addition to this, that inmate will have to spend a year or more in administrative segregation. Usually when inmates get frustrated, they take their frustrations out among each other because the consequences are less severe.

As I said earlier, working in a prison can sometimes be stressful for guards (but not most of the time). So, this leads to the question of how do guards vent their stress and frustration? They are required by the rules to maintain a professional attitude at all times. But there are subtle, hidden, and diabolical ways that they can vent their frustrations against the inmates. In many cases, inmates are not the direct cause of the guard's stress or frustrations. Nevertheless, inmates are the perfect scapegoat to unleash their fury upon. This is where the abuse of authority comes in at on the part of the C.O.'s.

Abuse of authority seldom comes from one place. There can be many reasons why this happens. My intention here is not to give a psychological profile of all of the mental and emotional illnesses that causes a person to abuse their authority. But the first assumption made by prisoners is that the guard must have been mistreated somewhere in his or her lifetime or that they have a low self esteem combined along with the fact that their life out on the streets must be miserable. Also, inmates say that the guards must get pleasure out of seeing them stressed out and suffering, and therefore the guard must be sadistic or either prejudice. The psychological warfare that goes on among inmates and guards is astounding in itself. The guards are trained to simply look upon all inmates as criminal. The correctional officers literally feel that they have moral authority over prisoners and can do what they feel, and this is where the abuse authority comes in again.

The trust factor among inmates and guards is almost nonexistent. Inmates ae all considered to be convicts. And the guards are looked at by the inmates as agents of the state, and the state is considered as crooked and unfair. Therefore, the guards are always questioning the intentions of the inmates and vice versa. Therefore, every new rule that comes out is looked upon as another measure to further restrict the little freedom that the inmates do have. The inmates virtually have no win with the guards and a lot of guards use this to their advantage to do whatever they want to the inmates. I am not insinuating here that it is only the guard's fault because I am well aware that the inmates play their negative part in this also. But the inmates do not have the authority so they will always receive the short end of the stick. In these situations, the guards always come out on top.

There have been many psychological studies that ascertain that humans have a tendency to abuse their authority when they are in absolute control over someone else. Even worse in this scenario is the fact that guards feel they have a moral duty to society to treat inmates the way that they do. Many times, this control is taken too far. The worse will come out of a person's character when they are given unchecked authority. What rights do prisoners have anyway? This is the mentality of a lot of guards. And even those few constitutional rights that inmates are given are constantly violated on a regular basis. These rights are merely looked at as a piece of paper to the guards, just something that the legislature did to make it appear as justice to society. The only time prisoner's rights are taken seriously is when they take their grievances to court and the guards and prison administrators have to answer to a higher authority.

Why does a human being lose so many of his or her rights after being convicted of a crime? I have studied many of the rights that prisoners supposedly have and, in my opinion, many of the harsh rules and regulations that prisoners have to submit to are very harsh. I agree the prisoners have to be monitored and subjected to some form of control for security purposes. But they should not be treated as subhuman by the mere fact that they have been convicted of a crime. The guards view it as their moral duty to be hard upon inmates. Their conscience is not too much bothered by this harsh treatment of this diabolical group of people (i.e. prisoners). But have they ever taken time to contemplate on the fact that maybe it is them being diabolical and cruel in their treatment of the prisoners?

In most countries' prisoners are supposed to have rights. In fact, these rights have been put in the law books of these countries. But in most cases, that is all that they become is a piece of paper. The guards as well as the prison administrators find countless ways to get around these rights. The only justification that the guards or administration needs to violate these rights are the pretense of security and safety measures. The courts have ruled that prisoner's rights may be violated if they will hinder the safety and security of the institution or the guards. This justification given by the courts is often abused by the guards. But 90 percent of the times that guards do abuse their authority never make it to a courtroom to be determined by a judge. At the least, a prisoner will file a grievance with the prison administration which routinely get denied and most prisoners leave it at that. The surprising thing about it is the fact that prisoners have more reading and studying time than anyone, but the majority of them are not even aware of their own rights. The guards are aware of this fact that they seldom have to answer to anyone about violating the rights of prisoners. The guard's word will usually always be believed over the inmates in 97 percent of the cases.

The Repercussions of a Rule Infraction

Clearly it has been shown that the guards have unchecked authority when it comes to prisoner's and this authority can and does get regularly abused. For prisoners it is mind boggling how much authority the guards are given over them. The guards are in a vital position to play constant mind games as well as real games with the inmate's lives. For instance, the guards can always write a prisoner a conduct violation or rule infraction which can have serious repercussions for a prisoner. An inmate can be written a conduct violation for almost anything. It would be hard for people in the free world to understand why inmates get in so much trouble for so many petty things. An inmate can get anywhere from a day to a year in solitary confinement for talking too loud depending on the circumstances. Most prisons have a list of rule infractions that inmates may be cited for. These rules go from one to fifty. The more serious of these are murder, rape, and assault. By all standards, prison discipline is very harsh and sometimes draconian.

Solitary confinement (the hole) does serve as a deterrent. It is a powerful tool in the hand of prison administrators. When an inmate is found guilty of a rule infraction, he or she is subject to numerous sanctions. The most severe of these sanctions can be placement in solitary confinement for years and referral for prosecution. For being late to a scheduled appointment or failing to obey the order of a guard, an inmate can lose his visiting privileges for 30 to 60 days, lose his recreation privileges, or have his early parole date taken, etc. Also, inmates may get their televisions and radios taken for up to months at a time. There are dozens of sanctions that can be imposed upon an inmate as a result of being found guilty of a conduct violation. Of course, prisoners try to enjoy the little so-called freedom that they do have within the prison and therefore, they attempt to stay away from rule infractions if they can. The guards are aware of this fact and they use it to their advantage as a powerful psychological weapon to be used against the prisoners.

Chances to make parole are often circumvented due to rule infractions. The parole board looks at a prisoner's behavior while he is in prison and will assess that if he or she cannot stay out of trouble in prison, then they definitely will not be able to stay out of trouble in free society. Judges look at it in the same way. On account of rule infractions, millions of prisoners are denied parole. Within the prison system, prisoners are given certain privileges and some, if not all, of these privileges can be taken away as a result of rule infractions. A simple piece of paper has a lot of power and can cause serious losses to a prisoner. This is just one of the many ways that guards can abuse their authority over prisoners.

Treating Inmates as Subhuman

It's surprising the amount of guards that see themselves as superior to prisoners. It actually gets to the point of guards seeing the prisoners as subhuman. Where does this mentality stem from? As I said earlier in this chapter, the guards see it as their moral duty to oversee inmates. Many guard's consciences are not troubled over their mistreatment of prisoners because they feel that the inmates are deserving of this treatment. Inmates sometimes wonder do many of the guards have a conscience. Even the nice or fair seeming guards have to take the side of their fellow officers to keep their jobs or stay in favor with their co-workers.

Why are inmates looked upon as subhuman by most guards? Did not God create all men equal? All prisoners should not be looked upon as condemned souls. The guards look at prisoners as the lowest class of people on earth. When guards treat prisoners as animals, they are attempting to bring their status as that below of a human being.

When prisoners are constantly forced to strip search, they are made to feel subhuman. When men and women are forced naked into holding rooms and showers with strangers, they are psychologically made to feel subhuman. In their mental as well as physical abuse of prisoners the guards are again treating them as subhuman. The word sub means below, thus the guards look at prisoners as something below that of a human when they treat them as subhuman. Prisoners are adults and when they are treated as children, they are reduced to feeling like sub-humans. In conclusion, I hope that I have painted an accurate picture of how guards abuse their authority over prisoners.

Feeling Trapped

Chapter 9
Feeling Trapped

Everyone gets tired of hearing the same ol' sad song. But in prison you are forced to hear it whether you desire to or not. The tunes just keep playing over and over again. Prison is a very abnormal environment that is designed to make people feel trapped. It is difficult to adjust to, and there is no where to go but the everyday places that are situated on the few acres of the prison compound. Every function in prison requires sign in sheets, standing in long restless lines, and showing identification cards. Usually inmates have to have a movement pass to go anywhere within the prison. At school and other classes, you must have a pass to even go to the bathroom.

Many observers say that prison is designed to make a person feel subhuman. If so, it does have its desired affects at times. There are signs and posts everywhere to let a person know that their every movement is being monitored. Everywhere you look there are guard towers, electric fences, and barb wire to remind prisoners how trapped they really are.

People in free society sometimes wonder how prisoners keep their sanity. From the outside looking in, they say that living in prison would be too much for them and they could not take it, but we as human beings never know what we can endure until we actually have to go through it. Sometimes the very prisoners who are in these situations do not even know how they get through the turbulent times that they have to go through while they are incarcerated. They just call it being strong and getting through what they have to do. Others will say that their life has always been hard, so prison is just another tribulation that they have to go through. There can be so much negativity, envy, and strife that people on the outside will find it shocking. The strange part about it is that all of these bitter emotions are masked but are displayed in subtle ways.

It appears that every new policy that comes out imposes a further restriction and designed to make inmates feel even more trapped. Everywhere you go in prison you are being told what to do, where to do it, how to do it, and when to do it. If you do not abide these rules, you are subject to even further restricted movement and oppression by being placed in administration segregation (the hole). It is a place that no one really likes to be; unless they like being alone and need time to themselves to get away from the yard for whatever various reasons that they may have. Administrative segregation consists of being confined in a small cubicle room of 8 by 9, 23 hours a day. There is nothing to do but think, read, and exercise. Every prisoner faces the threat of administration because they could be placed there at any given time. How much more trapped can a person feel being confined to a small cell for various amounts of time.

Administrative segregation becomes the epitome of being trapped. A person can even become trapped in their mind after thinking the same thoughts and worrying about the same things over and over again. In a small room with just a bed, toilet, and sink there is little space to move around. The human body gets restless after sleeping and laying around in the bed all day. A restless and energetic body wants to move around, thus a person gets up and paces the floor. The sights are the same, the smells are the same, and the deafening noise is all the same. Under certain circumstances, the prison administration can place a prisoner in administrative segregation as long as they deem desirable under the pretext that he or she is a threat to the administration, other prisoners, or even themselves. The future can seem hard to see at times. There is really nothing to look forward to because when you wake up in the morning the first thing that your eyes set upon is the metal door or walls that serve as a constant reminder to you of how trapped you really are.

The only freedom that you are allowed is the freedom of your thoughts. The mind can go anywhere and does not have to be confined to the prison. Some prisoners choose to trap their own minds and become institutionalized.

Man was created to be free, not in bondage. It is a known fact that prison can be a torturing experience, but at the same time as I have said before it is only what the individual makes of it. When a prisoner keeps their sanity and allow their minds to see beyond the prison experience then he or she should be able to look forward to the future and plan ahead for better things. If he or she has many plans and goals and strive for them then they will go around many of the obstacles that the entrapment of prison was designed to set upon them.

Life is bigger than prison. It is so easy though to allow one's mind to become trapped along with their body while they are in prison. That is why it remains my belief that the ultimate battle of being in prison is not to allow one's mind to be trapped there while one is in the process of trying to gain freedom. The spiritual person will say that they are ever free because their spirit is with God while the state only has their body. There are many ways to combat feeling trapped whether one is spiritual or agnostic. For every problem there is a solution, prison is just such a negative place to be in. Even if you try to keep a positive attitude about your situation, there are always miserable people around who will do anything to steal your peace. Although prison is designed to make a person feel trapped, a prisoner must still see life outside of the box. Prison is just a place in time and the life that a prisoner is living is bigger than the prison that they are confined to.

How Families and Spouses
Do Time with Prisoners Also

Chapter 10

How Family and Spouses Do Time with the Prisoners

Prisoners do not do time alone. Their families and spouses also do time with them. Prior to being incarcerated prisoners were and still are someone's father, brother, uncle, grandfather, mother, sister, aunt tee, niece, nephew, or grandmother. Some of these people were the sole providers of their household. Anyone is going to miss their mother. All across the world there are millions of mothers who are incarcerated. In the family hierarchy, the mother holds the most important position. She is the maintainer of the household and without her presence, things are sure to be amiss. Even a substitute cannot sustain her place in the household.

Prisoners are still human beings and their family members and spouses miss them as such. The vast majority of prisoners have family that cares about them and they will be there to support them. This places a heavy burden on their families in the free world. The first thing that comes to mind is the financial constraints that incarceration places upon the free family members of prisoners. But there are greater burdens outside of this. The emotional burdens have the greatest impact upon the prisoners as well as their families. Incarceration does not only punish the prisoner, but it also punishes his family. In fact, sometimes incarceration is more painful for the prisoner's family than for the prisoner him/herself. When a person has been convicted of a crime and knows that they are going to prison, they mentally prepare themselves for what is ahead. Entering prison may be an unknown world for them, but no matter how much they dislike prison, it is a place that they know they will be forced to reside for the next few years or beyond. The only thing they can do is be strong and attempt to make the best of prison and use it to change their lives for the better. In the end, they know that prison is something they will have to deal with. As far as their family members, it is a totally different struggle. They may attempt to prepare themselves for their family member's absence, but when that person is actually gone, they will discover that their mental preparation actually left them unprepared to deal with what actually has to be dealt with.

Prisoners are not just nameless people who do not have family members that love, care about, and need them. They are not just lawless people who do not need to be loved. Many prisoners have children and when they go to prison, their children are left without a mother or father. Their absences have a greater affect upon their children than anyone else. Kids are not as understanding as adults, and they seldom understand when their family members are taken away from them.

Children need their parents and they are not accustomed to living without them. They want their parents to be the ones raising them. There is no one in the world that can take the place of someone's parents. Usually in these situations, an aunt tee or older sibling, or perhaps a grandmother will step in to take care of their child while the parent goes off to prison. The skyrocketing rate of incarceration plays a significant part in why there are so many single mothers raising children by themselves. It is especially hard when a child's mother is incarcerated. Kids really need their mothers more than anything, and we all can understand this. Women are being incarcerated at high rate these days. Furthermore, ninety percent of the women incarcerated do have one or more children. So, think of the effect that this has on society.

How does it affect a child when he or she grows up without his or her mother or father due to incarceration? There is really no explanation that is acceptable to a child except in those few rare cases in which something happened where the parents actually had to do what they did to protect themselves or their family.

The void of the child's parents being gone can turn into emptiness and this emptiness is painful and leads to anger. Who does the child blame? Ultimately, their parents. In some cases, the children will begin to act up in school or strike out at their caregivers. Later on in life they may begin to lash out at society. The incarceration of their parents and other family members has a detrimental effect on children. It begins to manifest itself in their misbehavior at home and school, as well as with their interactions with their peers.

The next family member this has the greatest effect upon is the spouse or significant other. In many cases, they become the sole provider for their incarcerated family member. The person who is incarcerated will lean on them more than anyone else. Their lover is not at home with them, so they have to do without the affection that regular couples are able to lavish each other with. They have to spend many lonely nights in bed. They are forced to suffer loneliness along with their spouse who is incarcerated.

Next on this list is the parents of the incarcerated prisoner. A lot of people are still young when they enter prison. In many cases, their parents are their sole support. Parents always tend to miss their children no matter how grown they are or where they are at. And the fact that they are in prison makes them antsy about their children's well-being. A mother's very nature is to protect her child and she feels hopeless when her child is in prison because she cannot be there to protect them against the dangers that they will face in prison. A mother's love is always intense. A mother counts down the days that her child will be in prison because she longs for her child to be home, and it eats a mother up inside that their child is confined in prison. Parents also do time along with their children who are in prison.

Last but not least, other family members such as brothers, sisters, nieces, nephews, uncles, aunt tees, and grandparents are seriously affected by the incarceration of their family members. Once you have been raised with someone and get used to their presence in your life, they are missed by you when they are gone.

Now the financial burdens can place a great hardship upon the family and friends of prisoners. Prisoners need money to get accessories inside of prison. Prices in the prison canteen are usually twice the price of things in the free world. It is the same way with the collect phone calls. Of course, people in prison try to keep in constant communication with their loved ones on the street. This is very expensive. In order to talk on the phone, prisoners have to call collect. The prices for collect calls from prison cost twice as much as collect calls on the streets. In fact, the prices are ridiculous. Telecommunication companies make billions of dollars from overcharging prisoners' families on the outside. The government also profits from these phone calls because the phone companies give them a kickback from these profits. Thus, prisoner's family members suffer serious setbacks due to collect calls. In addition, prisoners have to buy toiletries, food, televisions, radios, headphones, and a host of other accessories to make their time in prison as comfortable as possible. Also, in order for prisoner's family members to visit them, it cost a lot of money. Usually prisoners are sent to prisons that are hundreds of miles away from their homes. Federal prisoners are always sent to a prison that is in a different state than the one in which they lived. This adds on hotel fees and gas fees that can cost hundreds of dollars anytime the family members of prisoners go to visit them.

Prisoners like to get visits on a regular basis because it helps them to do their time better. Plus, in their absence, their family members like to come and see them as often as possible. In addition to all of this, billions of dollars are spent on legal expenses for prisoners across the world. There are countless other financial hardships that they have to suffer supporting their family members in prison.

I have outlined in this chapter only some of the ways that the family members and spouses do time along with their incarcerated loved ones. There are countless other ways in which this process takes place. The family members of prisoners share in all of their fears and hopes. They hurt along with them, and the prisoner pain can become their pain also. 1 out of every 4 people in society has a family member who is incarcerated. Therefore, prisoners do not do their time alone, the family members of people who are in prison also does time along with them.

Employment in Prison

Chapter 11
Employment in Prison

Neither slavery, nor involuntary servitude, except as a punishment for crime whereof the party shall have been duly convicted, shall exist within the United States or any place subject to their jurisdiction.

~United States Constitution, Amendment 13~

Constitutional amendments such as these exist across the world. Slavery is considered as legal if the parties have been convicted of crime. Prison pays its employees slave labor wages. Government and big business have come to see the open market that slave wages offer prisoners. Corporations are free to enter into contracts with prison authorities and operate their companies through the prison. They are not troubled with labor unions because prisoners cannot form unions. These corporations also do not have to worry about medical benefits because prison labor offers no medical benefits. Advantages such as these save these companies billions of dollars at the prisoner's expense.

Employment in prison is big business that ultimately profit corporations and not society nor the prisoners who are doing the work. In prison, prisoners vie with each other for jobs to get the small benefits and extra freedom that these jobs offer them. The small wages that they receive can be considered helpful in a booming prison economy. Many prisoners have never held meaningful employment before they were incarcerated. In the free world they can just quit their jobs at will, but in prison they cannot quit without repercussions. Therefore, employment for prisoners does have its benefits in that it teaches prisoners discipline and responsibility. Thus, it does prepare them to hold down future employment once they are released into society.

There are many other complexities inherent in the prison employment system. It can also be used as an oppressive regime. Some prisoners are required to put in hundreds of hours of work before they are eligible for parole. Many prisoners are forced to work. If they refuse to work, then they will be placed in administrative segregation (the hole) until they agree to work. Furthermore, prisoners have to endure working under extremely dangerous conditions. There have been hundreds of thousands of accidental deaths recorded that have been related to prison workplace employment. Also, annually there are millions of prison workplace injuries that are recorded across the world. In fact, many of these injuries go unreported and these prisoners receive inadequate medical attention. These are just some of the bad breaks of working in prison. The supervisors have unlimited authority to treat the prisoners however they want to treat them. After all, in the first analysis prisoners are property of the state. As such, the state can do what it wills with its property. It is common practice for prison employers to mistreat their employees.

The profits that are reaped as a result of prison slave labor is stupendous. Everyone from conglomerate to the government gets their products made and manufactured at prison facilities. Therefore, prison labor is being prostituted by all of these entities. Prison factory jobs pay prisoners anywhere from 8 to 14 cents an hour. So, for a whole day of work, a prisoner will receive an average of seventy-five cents. In the free world, these same jobs pay their employees $25 to $30 dollars an hour. Therefore, companies save billions of dollars by building factories inside of prisons and using prisoners as employees. Companies do not have to offer such costly benefits as pensions, retirement funds, 401k plans, etc. All of this is obsolete under their contract with prison administrators. So, it is no wonder why the prison industrial sector is one of the fastest growing business in the economic sector.

Besides all of this labor from prisoners is what keeps the prison afloat. Prisoners are primarily responsible for the maintenance and upkeep of the prison. If not for prison labor the prison administration would have to hire outside contractors which would cost the government billions of dollars. Prisoners do all the work except actually building the prison. But every piece of furniture used in the prison is made inside of prison factories. Prisoners manufacture their own soap; they manufacture their own cleaning supplies such as disinfectant, window cleanser, floor wax, liquid soap, and a host of other supplies. All of these things and more are made inside of prison factories. When anything needs repaired inside of prison, it is the prisoners who fix these things. In prison, you can locate all kinds of professional laborers who have been convicted of crimes. A small portion of the prison population were employed as laborers before they came to prison. There are certified welders, plumbers, certified electricians, cooks, chiefs, computer majors, homebuilders, construction workers, and the like inside of prison. These people easily obtain employment in these fields while they are in prison. Furthermore, other less experienced prisoners are trained on the job and hired in these vital positions.

Prisoners reinstall locks to the very cells that house them. When toilets get clogged, it is the prisoners themselves who unclog them. When the shower heads or anything is broken inside of the prison it is the prisoners themselves that fix all of these things. The maintenance supervisor just merely stands by and oversees, while prisoners do ninety-eight percent of the work that needs to be done.

Prisoners are used as clerks to keep inventory of everything that comes into and leaves out of the prison. They do all the work in the prison warehouse and canteen. It is the prisoners who do all of the cleaning throughout the entire prison. Prisoners manufacture their own clothing, distribute the clothing, as well as wash and press their own clothing. Prisoners cook and serve their own food. All of this self-labor from the prisoners saves the government billions of dollars. Prisoners are paid 8 to 14 cents an hour to be employed for these services in the prison. If prisoners across the world would go on strike and refuse to work for even a day, governments all over the world would lose billions of dollars in paying outside contractors to keep the prisons afloat and running.

It is clear by the evidence documented in this chapter that prison employment serves a meaningful purpose to the government and multi-billion-dollar corporations. But slave labor must be eliminated if the prison employment system is to really help in the rehabilitation process. Prisoners must not continue to be used as slaves. It becomes inherent in a slave's nature to rebel and this is why so many prisoners rebel against society after they are released.

Prison employment must begin to really be equal employment. It must upgrade itself in accord with the technological world that prisoners will face when they are released into the free world. The majority of prison jobs are mediocre and after a prisoner is released and has no real work experience, it plays a great part in why it is so difficult for ex-cons to get hired. In this modern technological world, many prisoners are lost when they get out. Their employment inside of the prison was not equipped enough to even begin to prepare them to hold down a meaningful job in today's modern technological employment market. Therefore, prison employment and job training must be upgraded so that it will meet the demands that today's job market calls for.

Solutions to the Problems Plaguing the World's Prisons

Chapter 12

Solutions to the Problems Plaguing the World's Prisons

Penalogist put forth the argument that we need reforms in the penal system. They act as if reforms will change or remedy the countless flaws that have become ingrained in criminal justice systems across the world. Reforms only deal with the surface of the problem and fails to offer any real solutions. Why is the recidivism rate so high? In an earlier chapter, I put forth convincing evidence that prison does not rehabilitate criminals. Today's prisons are more like warehouses that house people for economical reasons. The construction and maintenance of prisons is a multi-billion-dollar business. Poverty is the root cause of why most people are in prison. But the whole economic order of the world would have to be rearranged in order for us to eliminate poverty. Although the economic rearrangement of the world's economy would help us to eliminate poverty and in turn dramatically reduce the world's prison population, we have to narrow the scope in an effort to reduce the prison population to the more indirect and immediate causes of why ex-cons keep coming back to prison. For the record it must be stated that I do not claim to have expertise knowledge in this field nor do I present myself as a scholar in this arena, but as someone who deals with these problems on a personal level every day I feel qualified enough to outline a system by which prisoners can truly be rehabilitated and not come back to prison.

First and foremost, the criminal justice system needs to be dismantled and rebuilt on a sincere platform of justice. As it stands now, things are not fair, and the poor offenders always get harsher sentences than richer offenders who have committed far worse crimes than the poor. As things stand right now, the public appears to be satisfied with the criminal justice system, or should I say that the public is not disillusioned with the criminal justice system enough to want to dismantle it. Therefore, we must look to the criminal justice system as it stands right now and come up with creative ways to really change the criminal mentality that causes ex-prisoners to commit new crimes and go back to prison. Earlier in this book I pointed out the fact that all of the real helpful rehabilitative classes and programs have been removed from the majority of all prisons. These programs and classes must be reinstated if we are going to make any forward progress in sincerely rehabilitating prisoners. Programs must be implemented that truly offer prisoners a different way of life to live once they are released back into society.

We must ask ourselves, what do most prisoners have to go home to once they are released? Most of them will return to the same crime ridden neighborhoods that they came from. Some of the very houses they will return to are crime infested households. How can they escape such temptation when it surrounds them everywhere that they turn in their neighborhoods? What skills has prison taught them to deal with the temptations that they will face once they are released? Prison alone does not teach them anything except to value their freedom. This alone will not help them stop committing crimes once they are released. Their whole criminal mentality must be reversed. The ultimate question is how can this be done? Prisoners must be offered better opportunities to change the course of their life once they are released. What are prisoners offered when they first go to prison? Nothing. Prisoners are just bunched together in cells or dorms and left at their own whim with guards overseeing them for security reasons only. Diagnostic centers must be built on the model of really assessing the needs of each prisoner as he or she comes through the door. There must be prisons that cater to certain problems that each class of prisoners suffer from. There must be such classes that deal with child abuse, domestic abuse, etc. All of these problems must be asked of new prisoners through questionnaires and counselors. Diagnostic centers are so overburdened and crowded that such needs of prisoners are not assessed and taken seriously. But it is these needs that should be dealt with that will help us to truly rehabilitate prisoners. As long as such underlying issues like this exist, then we all risk the chance of these men getting back into society committing new crimes. For those prisoners who have committed violent crimes, we have to truly determine why are they violent? Since many of them are violent in society, we have to determine why they choose not to be violent while they are in prison. What makes them click? What triggers their violent reactions to simple situations in society that could have been resolved in a much easier and simple manner?

Everything that happens in a person's childhood affects them as an adult. Most prisoners had a very hard childhood. Many of their problems stem from their childhood. A lot of them have never healed from their childhood scars and judging by their actions it appears that a lot of prisoners are living in their second childhood, meaning that they have not developed into an adult state of mind. The same problems that they had to deal with during their childhood are the same problems that plague them today. Therefore, when prisoners come in the door, these issues must be addressed, and there must be classes as well as programs that help prisoners to combat the illnesses that plague them.

Violence becomes a cycle of life for many prisoners due to the violence that was inflicted upon them as children. The cycle must stop. Prison can only inflame such violent tendencies in these men if prison does not help them to suppress their violent inclinations. Being incarcerated in prison is frustrating and can build up a lot of rage in a person. If this negative energy is not properly channeled, it can have detrimental effects for the prisoner, as well as the society into which he or she will be released. There must be violent prevention programs established in every phase of the prison system. In accord with this, the penal authorities must establish a classification system by which prisoners will be sent to certain prison facilities that address their particular needs. We must start dealing with the root causes of the particular problems that individual prisoners have. For instance, a drug program that fails to tackle the root cause of an inmate's substance abuse serves no real purpose. It merely becomes a class that a prisoner attends to pass time or merely to obtain a certificate. The failure of the criminal justice system is apparent. It attempts to deal with the surface of the problem, and this leads to failure every time. If you fail to cut the roots of the weeds, then they will surely reappear. In the same instance, if we fail to dig to the root of the problems that plague the world's prisoners, they are most likely to commit new crimes and end up back in prison. Who do we blame? We must ultimately blame the criminal justice system because the blame lies with them. Why? Prisoners can be rehabilitated, but the system is failing to rehabilitate them. Fighting crime is not a losing battle. Most prisoners want to be rehabilitated but all they know is how to get by the way in which they were raised in their environments. In prison they learn even more desperate survival skills. But many of these are used in a negative way.

What better place for a person to truly change their life than in prison? Truly prison provides an almost perfect set up for them to be able to clearly see their mistakes and begin to change their ways. Despite all of its flaws, prison is a place where a person is allowed ample time to think about past mistakes and try to remedy them. Prison is a place where a person can truly focus if he or she desires to do so. Away from all of the madness and chaos they participated in on the streets, they are offered a chance to see life through clear eyes not befogged by the intoxicated state they lived in on the outside. Prisoners have ample time to read and study to broaden their horizon as well as learn many new things. Whatever gifts or talents they possess can be fully developed and bought to perfection during the time that they are in prison. So, despite its flaws, prison does have its advantages. But these advantages are often taken for granted and do not mean anything if they are not used for positive purposes.

Prisons are overcrowded and the staff is overburdened. Prisoners are not dealt with on an individual or even group level; they are dealt with as a prison mass. Meaning that they are simply pushed through the system with no real acknowledgement to their individual needs. Prisoners are not paid any attention until they get in trouble or engage in anti-authority activities. Beyond this, they are just a nameless person within the prison population. Whatever may be going on in their personal life is irrelevant to prison authorities as long as it does not affect the security of the institution. This very ignorance of the prisoner's individual needs is what leaves this issue not dealt with and ultimately causes prisoners to commit new crimes and come back to prison. There must be more programs established within the prison system that helps prisoners deal with the certain things that affect their lives. First this must be done on a group level and in turn there must be certain mechanisms within that group system that gives individual attention to the problems of the prisoners within the group.

Rehabilitation is an intense process. It is not something that can happen by placing people in a prison warehouse and leaving them there on their own whim. Prisoners are people in our society who have violated the laws of society and thus they need to be corrected so they may reenter back into society as better citizens. As long as we cast them away in prison and pay their progress, no attention then nothing will change about them and they will enter into society as the same people who they were before they went to prison. During the time they were cast away in prison, they cost taxpayers billions of dollars under the pretext that they were being rehabilitated when they really were not. As things stand now, we have a broken criminal justice system that does not fix any of the broken elements of our society. It only breaks them further apart. Even a broke machine can operate well enough to manufacture some of the products that it has been built to manufacture. As I said earlier, the entire criminal justice system needs to be dismantled and built on a true foundation of justice for the poor as well as the rich. But as I also pointed out the fact that the majority of the public seems to be content with the system and the results that it is producing. A whole new political conscious would have to be ingested into the minds of the public in order for us to dismantle the entire criminal justice system and rebuild it. Since that does not seem likely, we must work to act on our own to really produce the necessary measures that will help us to rehabilitate prisoners and make changes in the penal system that addresses the problems of the inmates that are there and helps them to change. I am not a reformist, nor a pacifist, I am a realest though. Therefore, as things stand now, that is why I am arguing for us to just do what we can now to really help prisoners to change their lives.

The problems that affect our system such as overcrowding leaves us just shuffling people through the prison system as a number lost in the system until it is time for them to go up for parole. Then we have to ask ourselves what criteria do prisoners have to meet in order for them to make parole? What are the things that they have to do to qualify for parole? The mediocre criteria that the average parole board is now asking for does not produce any meaningful results in ex-prisoners once they are released back into free society. And as such, prison has served them no meaningful purpose. They were just put away for a few years with no real lesson learned. If the parole boards really served any real purpose, the recidivist rate wouldn't be so high. I am not arguing that prisoners should be kept in prison for longer amounts of time. I am arguing that the whole parole system be revamped. Parole eligibility needs to be based on a whole different criterion. The present structure of the parole board is severely flawed. I am speaking about parole boards all over the world. The structure of the world's parole boards must be made to coincide with the agendas of these programs to truly rehabilitate prisoners. Only then will the parole board be serving its purpose.

Again, it must be stressed that I am not a reformist, so I do not just specifically argue for changes within a system that I feel is corrupted from the bottom up. But since the mass public for all intents and purposes seem to be content with the present make up of this system, then we have to work with what we can to begin to rehabilitate our prisoners and send them into society as changed persons. This is not a legal text or a judicial essay, so I will not make it into either one as I put forth solutions that help us to change the results of the problems that plagues prisons all across the world. Therefore, I will not point out each flaw within the system that needs to be changed. I have just given a brief overview of some of the things that need to be changed or added on to in order for us to produce the needed results within the present criminal justice system. These solutions are concrete and can have successful results if implemented. The above and countless other changes presented by penologists, psychologists, social workers, and others need to be implemented in order for us to reach true solutions to the problems that plague the world's prisons.

A Conviction Designed for Greatness

When a person is convicted of a crime, greatness is the last thing on their mind. Freedom is what they are thinking about constantly. But in time, they come to realize that freedom is a state of mind. So, they begin to pursue mental freedom. Through this quest, a prisoner comes to see that prison is not their greatest burden. Via their studies, they come to see that they, the truly free, are people that are great or at least striving for greatness. Thus, a seed is born. From the depths of the dirt, the convicted person starts striving for their own greatness. It is from the lowest depths that the greatest people have risen. That's even true for people in prison.

During pre-biblical days, Joseph rose from the rank of prisoner to one of the highest state officials in Egypt. While in prison, he had a vision, as do many of us who still sit in prison. There are countless examples of many men who were convicted of a crime; then found their true calling in life and then rose to greatness. In contemporary times, we have Malcolm X, Merle Haggard, and Nelson Mandela as examples. Yet many of us have potential to rise to some level of greatness. Yet as the saying goes: many are called, but few are chosen. Meaning that many can potentially be called to greatness, but only a few will do the necessary hard work and make the needed sacrifice to achieve greatness in life or in their particular calling or field.

From the conviction of a crime, a man can become convicted of his own potential for greatness. Let's look at the word conviction.

Conviction (1) the act of convicting a person in court; (2) the state of being convinced; (3) a strong persuasion or belief.

After being convicted of a crime in court, the prisoner must use his time to find himself; thereby finding his true calling in life. We all have a gift, something that we can contribute to the world. A prisoner must be convinced of this. His strong belief in his own redemption will lead him to a path of maturity and growth.

Once a person has been down for so long, he wants to rise to unknown heights. If he doesn't limit his vision, he can surely attain greatness. It's been said that the mind can achieve what the mind can conceive. This can be done even from a prison cell. In fact, it has been done time and time again as documented throughout history. Certainly, a criminal conviction is not designed to help a person achieve greatness. Designed conviction is when a prisoner personally designs their conviction to change their life for the better.

To construct such a design takes great conviction on the part of the prisoner. It requires a strenuous effort. Once the seed of greatness is implanted in the mind of the prisoner, he must till the soil in order for the seed to germinate. This seed is watered through reading books and other materials. The sun shines on the seed through inspirational tidbits such as motivational music and encouraging movies. During the work to change his life is the air that allows his tree to blossom. Programs, classes, college, creating non-profits, blueprints for charity, etc., is the nutrients that nurture the seed of greatness. Look at Malcolm

X and how he designed his conviction to become great. The average prisoner must also design his conviction to attain to greatness. Take the worse situation of your life and become your best self. There is greatness in you if you search for it by design. If you succeed in finding it then you can transform your personal situation from the worst to the best. Then you can turn your entire life around as a result of a designed conviction.

Doing A Life Sentence While
Serving Life Behind Bars

Chapter 13

Doing A Life Sentence
While Serving Life
Behind Bars

Two out of ten prisoners are serving a life sentence. In their book "The Meaning of Life" by Marc Mauer and Ashley Nellis, and of The Sentencing Project, these authors detail the significant rise of life sentences being handed out. Serving prison time is very difficult but it is even harder when you are serving a life sentence. Whatever indignities you are suffering is endless. People who are serving a short prison sentence at least know that they're suffering in prison will one day come to an end. Not so for the lifers. Worse still is that times in prison can get worse. So you are not afforded the mental relief of other prisoners who can at least say that "one day soon this will be over." for the life is it will never be over until they die.

Living with the mental burden of knowing that you are never going home is tough. Tougher still is the mental torture of knowing all the simple joys of the free world that you will never get to experience again. Harsh as it may seem, I have repeated numerous times throughout this book life indeed does go on inside prison. What can a lifer do but continue to live his/her life. I know from experience because I serve as a lifer. Even when a lifer makes parole, he/she is still serving that life sentence while on parole. Therefore, that life sentence still hangs over their head. Imagine the burden of walking around on the streets while still serving a life sentence with one foot in and one foot out. (That's a whole other subject for another day, time, and place.)

Throughout this text I have warned against a person becoming institutionalized. Although I am a lifer, I always fought against being institutionalized mentally. I refused to become this way. I had to live my best life while serving life and I adhere other lifers to do so as well. This is a niche group of prisoners serving a living death sentence behind bars. For informational purposes it should also be noted that not all of them are locked up for violent crimes. A lot of lifers only have drug charges. Another substantial chunk of these lifers were juveniles while they committed their crimes. Others were women who were battered and abused by their spouses. The list of mitigating circumstances is endless, nevertheless they are serving a life sentence.

In prison, as in the free world, all you can do is wake up each morning; put one foot in front of the other one and keep it moving. In here life goes on. Lifers with ambition spend a lot of their time trying to get their life sentence overturned. They are constantly trying to figure out a way to get their life sentence reduced so they can somehow go home one day. It is hard being away from your family as well as everything you have left behind. It feels like you have lost everything, but even as a lifer you still have a lot to lose. More importantly, you can lose your life's purpose if you don't claim it. You must take hold of your life and find meaning in it while serving life. Make the life sentence serve you while you are serving life.

How? You accomplish this by doing something worthwhile with your time. View your life as still having significant meaning. Contribute to the world in whatever positive way that you can, even from your jail cell. Never give up.

Maximum Security vs. Minimum Security

I have served over two decades in maximum security prison. I have served a minimum amount of time in a minimum-security prison as well. There is a world of difference between the two prisons settings. For one, maximum security prisoners are serving a more significant amount of time. This results in more strict lock down as well as stricter rules that come with increased security controls. With that said, of course, there is ten times more violence in maximum security prisons.

As a result, the environment in a maximum is more disciplined whereas chaos runs rampant at minimum security prisons. At a maximum, the prisoners act as if they have something serious on their minds, while at a minimum-security prison the overall population has a nonchalant care-free attitude. There is always tension at a maximum while the potential for serious violence is ever present. Knives are carried or hidden every few yards. At the minimum-security camps, knives are very seldom used or even accessed because nobody there wants to intentionally lose their release date.

However, minimum security prisons are notorious for taking inmates release dates. Relative minor conduct rule violations can get your release date postponed for up to 90 days or six months. If your urine tests positive for drug usage you will lose your release date for maybe a year or so. Nowadays the guards lock up inmates for looking visibly high or intoxicated. Once they take you to solitary confinement for what they call a visual (appearing to be visibly intoxicated), there is a 90% chance that they will take your original release date. I witnessed prisoners losing release dates every day while at a minimum-security prison. A lot of the things that inmates get in trouble for at a minimum-security prison is something that guards wouldn't even bat an eye at in a maximum-security prison. That's why we say that it is real petty at minimum security prisons. You have virtually no privacy there while at a maximum security you are closed in a private cell. Minimum security prisons are mostly open dormitories or 10-man cells.

The caveat of a minimum-security prison is that there is 10 times more freedom than at a maximum-security prison. This is because the lower security levels are designed to prepare inmates for freedom. There are more programs and vocational classes for the prisoners as well. Serious violence is at an all-time low at minimum security also. Therefore, there are pros and cons at both maximum- and minimum-security prisons. The difference between these two worlds is endless. I just wanted to give the reader a small window to look inside the different worlds of prison.

Other Books by Bobby Bostic

Dear Mama: The Life and Struggles of a Single Mother

Generation Misunderstood: Generation Next

Mind Diamonds: Shining on Your Mind

Mental Jewelry:

Wear It on Your Brain

When Life Gives You

lemons:

Make Lemonade

Time: Endless Moments

In Prison

Also look for future books, products, and
merchandise by Bobby Bostic.

Printed in Great Britain
by Amazon

20140892R00106